The Brontës
Children of the Moors

By Mick Manning and Brita Granström

W

FRANKLIN WATTS

LONDON • SYDNEY

The Brontës
Children of the Moors

I once met a lady up on a windy moor and she told me a story I'll never forget; it's a story I'm going to pass on to you. But let's start at the beginning: I grew up in Haworth, a small moorland village in Yorkshire, where the famous Brontë sisters had lived long ago. One day, when I was about 8, the BBC came to our village school looking for someone to play the part of a shepherd boy, frightened by ghosts, for a new TV series of Emily Brontë's *Wuthering Heights*. They chose me! Filming day found me sitting on the moor, waiting for my turn on camera, feeling a bit nervous. The wind was whispering through the heather so gently that I think I nodded off. I woke to find a lady wearing old-fashioned clothes lying next to me. She smiled and said, "I don't think Emily would have wanted you to be frightened of ghosts." And with that she began her story . . .

Charlotte's Story 1820

"A ruffled mind makes a restless pillow." Charlotte Brontë

My name is Charlotte. Come back with me to the spring of 1820, when my father, Patrick Brontë, became the new parson of the moorland parish of Haworth, Yorkshire. Birds were singing as we crossed the Pennine Hills in a procession of heavily laden carts, containing my whole family and everything we owned. There was my father, my mother and my sisters (Maria, Elizabeth, Emily, baby Anne), my brother, Branwell, and not forgetting our servants, Sarah and Nancy Garrs. After ten steep, scrambling miles of muddy tracks we arrived at our new home: Haworth Parsonage.

The people of Haworth could be hard to please. A previous vicar had been driven out of the village after a local man rode into the church, sitting backwards on a donkey, to screams of laughter from the rowdy church goers.

We heard a mistle thrush singing in the churchyard: a sign of spring.

Haworth people worked mostly in the cloth industry or farming. The town's drinking water was filthy: it either drained through the overcrowded graveyard or was polluted by outside toilets, causing deadly diseases such as cholera. Almost half of local children died before the age of six.

The Parsonage 1820

"But what on earth is half so dear; So longed for as the hearth of home?" Emily Brontë

My first impression of our new home was a warm kitchen with a blazing fire. Then, after supper, a winding staircase that led us past windows that looked towards the open moor. We girls soon found our bedroom. That night, after Sarah had tied rags in our hair (to keep our ringlets), we fell asleep with the window open, listening to the tolling of the church bells and the gentle calls of curlews from the moor.

I wonder what's upstairs?

At first us older girls shared a front bedroom that looked out over the graveyard, the church and the village rooftops beyond. Behind our house stretched the open moor.

7

Around Haworth 1821-24

"We have just seen something of the mighty power of God: he has unsheathed his sword and brandished it over our heads ..." Patrick Brontë, on the Crow Hill Bog Burst

In 1821, after months of illness, our dear mother died, leaving my father heart-broken. It was a terrible time. Our aunt Elizabeth moved into the parsonage to look after us and our maid Sarah began to take us everywhere with her, from shopping trips down the steep, cobbled hill to brisk walks up on the moor. In 1824, I was sent to boarding school with my older sisters, Maria and Elizabeth, and missed a great calamity – the Crow Hill Bog Burst.

You are safe now, children.

One day, Sarah was out with Emily, Anne and Branwell when a torrential thunderstorm caused a great landslide on the boggy moorland of Crow Hill. When father felt the deep rumble shake the house, he thought it was the end of the world. Taking his pistol, he went to look for his children and found them sheltering in the doorway of Ponden Hall, a moorland manor house.

9

Cowan Bridge School 1824-25

"What a face he had... what a mouth! and what large prominent teeth!" Charlotte Brontë describes a headmaster in *Jane Eyre*

I was so excited to go to school – there was so much to learn and discover. My high hopes were dashed though when I realised the teachers, led by the school's founder, the Reverend Carus Wilson, were bullies, picking especially upon my sister Maria. The food was inedible, the buildings were cold and damp and, by February, poor Maria was very ill. She was sent home, but it was too late; she died of tuberculosis in May, just as the hawthorn was blossoming on the moor. Then Elizabeth became ill... Father came and fetched us away from that terrible place, but within a few weeks Elizabeth was also laid to rest.

All schools cost money in those days and most schools were beyond Father's means. When he heard about the low-priced Clergy's Daughter's Boarding School he thought it a godsend, enrolling Maria and Elizabeth first and then me a few months later. Emily joined us that autumn.

Every Sunday that winter, we pupils were marched along a muddy, and often snowy, riverside path to church. We had to sit for hours in wet shoes and clothes, with no heating, listening to Reverand Wilson's terrifying sermons warning that God would punish naughty little girls.

11

Imaginary Worlds 1825-27

"'It was spring, and the skylark was singing;' Those words they awakened a spell." Emily Brontë

After the tragic loss of our sisters, Father taught us at home. Our aunt instructed us in needlework and we also enjoyed art and piano lessons. Emily and I shared a bedroom by then and, one morning, we woke to find a beautiful wooden village beside our beds. We'd just called Anne when Branwell rushed in, holding a box of painted soldiers! Our kind father had bought us these presents. We each chose a soldier and invented four kingdoms for our "young men" to rule. The Great Glass Town Confederacy was born: an imaginary world controlled by giant super-beings called the four Genii – us! Talli (me), Branii (Branwell), Emmii (Emily) and Annii (Anne).

Mine's Bonaparte!

This is the Duke of Wellington!

Mine looks so serious. Let's call him Gravey.

Mine shall be called Waiting Boy!

At first, we didn't write down the Glass Town adventures. They were a wild game that even involved the servants. One day, playing a prince escaping battle, our servant Sarah climbed out of a window and broke a branch of Father's favourite cherry tree!

As we grew older, Sarah and her sister left the parsonage and a local woman, Tabby, came to keep house. She told us many local stories and legends that left a deep impression on all of us.

The Islanders and Beyond 1827-31

"We wove a web in childhood, a web of sunny air; We dug a spring in infancy of water pure and fair."
Charlotte Brontë

One dark night, we'd been sitting round the kitchen fire as a snowstorm shook the house. Tabby had told us to go to bed early to save candles but Branwell grumbled, "I'd rather do anything than that." So, before we went to bed, we each imagined an island of our own and chose a leader – a new game had begun. We were all living more and more inside our imaginary worlds and we started to write down and illustrate our stories. My kingdom was full of nobles and royalty set in a tropical climate. In contrast, Emily's was more ordinary; more like home. My story, *A Day at Parry's Palace*, is just one of many, many stories we wrote back then. It is full of jokes and pokes gentle fun at Emily's land.

A DAY AT PARRY'S PALACE 1830 by Charlotte (aged 14)

My hero, Lord Charles Wellesley, goes to visit Emily's land and the palace of her hero, Captain Parry.

What a curious country!

Instead of the tall, warlike people of his own kingdom, Charles sees factory workers in blue jackets and brown dresses.

Hello Sir!

At the palace, Charles is greeted by Sir Edward Parry and his wife. They bring in "Little Eater", their noisy child dressed in a greasy pinafore! There is a feast of beef, Yorkshire pudding and apple pie.

One guest gets such terrible indigestion the Genius Emii (Emily) has to be summoned. She makes him better with a magic spell and then vanishes.

I found my visit intolerably dull!

The next morning Lord Charles travels home to Glass Town thinking his own kingdom is a much, much better place!

Emily and I even had secret plays we called "bed plays" and they were very nice ones too.

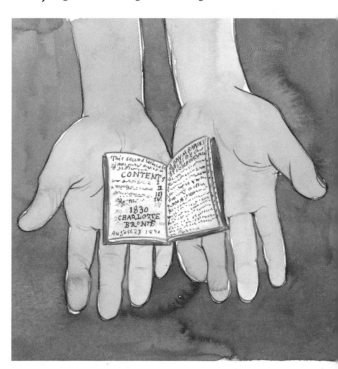

We began to write down our stories around 1829, and from then on began to spend our free hours creating tiny, toy-soldier-sized magazines, newspapers and booklets.

Roe Head 1831

"We thought her very ignorant, for she had never learnt grammar at all, and very little geography."
Mary Taylor, a school friend, on Charlotte's arrival at Roe Head

As we grew older, our imaginary worlds grew more complex. Branwell and I created Angria, while Emily and Anne, fed up of being bossed about by their big brother and sister, created Gondal. Our stories featured love affairs, executions, murders and imprisonments! My hero was often the Duke of Wellington, the great British general. I gave him imaginary sons but there was also the warlike Julius Brenzaida, not to mention the debonair Duke of Zamorna. Then, in January 1831, I was sent to Roe Head, a very nice boarding school run by a kind lady called Miss Wooler. But my stories didn't stop, I continued them in my letters home.

I soon made new friends at Roe Head, such as lovely Ellen Nussey and Mary Taylor. At night, we thrilled to hear spine-tingling rustling noises on the staircase and imagined a ghostly lady prowling the corridor! I did so well at Roe Hall that I finished my lessons in 18 months and was able to go home again. Later, I would return there as a teacher.

Exploring the Moors

"Speak of the North! A lonely moor ..." Charlotte Brontë

We still missed our sisters deeply and, as the seasons turned, we continued our childhood habit of long walks on the blustery moors. We found comfort there together, amid the heather and the harebells. We picked up feathers and found curlew nests, we spotted shy lizards and noisy lapwings. We buzzed like bees and chattered like skylarks, losing ourselves in our secret world, a world of dashing heroes and scheming villains that went with us everywhere. Many of our poems were composed up on the moor, long before we wrote them down.

Let's hear Charlotte's new poem.

Speak of the North! A lonely moor ...

Silent and dark and trackless swells ...

18

The waves of some wild streamlet pour Hurriedly through its ferny dells.

Looking back, perhaps our imaginary world helped us come to terms with the deaths of our dear mother and sisters and somehow provided an escape; an inner world we shared.

Feathers of Moorland Birds

Lapwing feather

Snipe feather

Red grouse feather

Father would often read us stories of travel and history as well as his own poetry and family tales. Many of our heroes were inspired by these stories. That's how I learnt about the Duke of Wellington and his victory at the Battle of Waterloo. Father usually went to bed at 9pm and as we grew older we would stay up and walk around the dining table making up stories as we went.

Ellen's Visit 1833

"My sister Emily loved the moors. Flowers brighter than the rose bloomed in the blackest of the heath for her." Charlotte Brontë

When my school friend Ellen came to Haworth, we showed her our favourite place on the moor, called the meeting of the waters – I hear they call it Brontë Waterfall now. It was a lovely day; Ellen helped Branwell make stepping-stones while Anne, Emily and I sat on the little packhorse bridge daydreaming. Emily loved the moors even more than the rest of us. She felt free there in that wild solitude. On the way back, Emily pointed out birds to Ellen as they flapped up under the nose of our Irish terrier, Grasper, who forged ahead through the deep heather, guiding us home.

While we were there, Emily found some tadpoles and dabbled her fingers among them, naming them brave or cowardly according to how they swam.

Emily loved animals. She once found a merlin sitting in the heather, injured perhaps by a gamekeeper's gun. Despite her hands getting scratched by its sharp talons, Emily took the falcon home and named it Nero. It soon became her dear pet.

Romantic Ruins 1833

"An excursion becomes quite a different thing when there are gentlemen of the party."
Charlotte Brontë, *Shirley*

At the end of Ellen's visit, we put our pocket money together and Branwell hired a carriage to take us all to the ruins of Bolton Abbey, a romantic beauty spot. Branwell was charming and gave Ellen and the rest of us a guided tour. It was a wonderful day out; and like many of our real-life experiences it inspired us all to think up still more events in our imaginary kingdoms.

Such romantic ruins certainly inspired my imagination: years later, I would write in Jane Eyre; "Winter snows, I thought, had drifted through that void arch, winter rains beaten in at those hollow casements."

Branwell had never been to Bolton Abbey before, but, being so clever, he had read and memorised all the details beforehand and gave us all the facts. He made a thrilling tour guide.

Branwell led us over the famous stepping-stones and we made up romantic adventures among the ruins before Ellen's family came to collect her.

23

One day, your painting may be famous, Branwell.

Branwell 1834

*"... some may quite forget thy name; But my sad heart must ever mourn
Thy ruined hopes, thy blighted fame!"* Emily Brontë

In 1834, Branwell painted our group portrait, and he did it beautifully.
We all felt he could become a famous painter and that he should apply
to the Royal Academy School in London. I'm not sure what happened,
but he never went to study there. My talented brother – he had a
brilliant mind and so wanted to be either an artist or a poet; but alas,
for one reason or another, things never seemed to work out for him.

Branwell became a portrait painter in the
local town of Bradford, only to return to
Haworth in 1839. Then he became a private
tutor; first in the Lake District and, later, in
a position near York where our sister Anne
already worked.

Between tutoring jobs Branwell worked as a
railway clerk. But he was sacked after his
railway account books were found to have errors
and to be covered with poems and doodles.

Emily 1838

"For the moors where the linnet was trilling Its song on the old granite stone; Where the lark – the wild skylark was filling Every breast with delight like its own." Emily Brontë

In September 1838, Emily became a teacher at Law Hill School near Halifax, often working from six in the morning until late at night. Such long days must have felt like a prison sentence to Emily and made her pine for the freedom of her beloved moorland. When the day was done she would write poetry, including what would become one of her most famous poems, 'A Little While'. After only six months, Emily left the school and went home to Haworth.
There she spent her time helping Tabby with the housekeeping and training their new guard dog, a huge mastiff named Keeper.

A Little While (extracts)

A little while, a little while,
The weary task is put away,
And I can sing and I can smile,
Alike, while I have holiday.

There is a spot, 'mid barren hills,
Where winter howls, and driving rain;
But, if the dreary tempest chills,
There is a light that warms again.

The house is old, the trees are bare,
Moonless above bends twilight's dome;
But what on earth is half so dear –
So longed for – as the hearth of home?

The mute bird sitting on the stone,
The dank moss dripping from the wall,
The thorn-trees gaunt, the walks o'ergrown,
I love them – how I love them all!'

This poem shows how much dear Emily missed Haworth, even in the dreariest winter weather. Just like the wild birds that returned to nest on the moor each spring, so she spread her wings and returned home.

Curlew

Skylark   Lapwing

On the moors in spring, curlews have a beautiful, lonely, bubbling call. Lapwings flap and dive with a husky "peewit". Skylarks sing their hearts out as they climb higher and higher.

27

Brussels 1842

"All my heart is yours, sir: it belongs to you; and with you it would remain..."
Charlotte Brontë, *Jane Eyre*

Emily and I had a dream of starting our own school, but first we needed more experience. In 1842, I persuaded Emily to come with me to study and also teach part-time at the Madame Heger's School for Young Ladies in Brussels, Belgium. We'd been there eight months when a letter from home told us our aunt had died. We rushed home to be with Father and share his grief. Emily stayed to look after him but I returned to Brussels. I was so lonely, far away, without my sister, that I began to fall in love with my teacher. But Mr Heger was a happily married man and would not return my feelings, so in 1844 I left Brussels forever. Back home, Mr Heger haunted my thoughts. I sent him many heartfelt letters from Haworth. I was lovesick and walked the moors in the wildest of weather, dreaming of him.

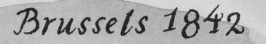

Welcome to Belgium!

Brussels, the capital of Belgium, was crowded with fashionable and clever people, not least Constantin Heger, my inspiring teacher. I fell head over heels for him but, though flattered, he gave me no encouragement.

After my walks, cold and tearful, I would change in the scullery. Slowly my lovesickness began to fade. Emily and I advertised our school, the Misses Brontë's Establishment at the Parsonage, but not one pupil applied and our dream had to be abandoned.

Anne 1845

"If we can only speak to slander our betters, let us hold our tongues."
Anne Brontë, *The Tenant of Wildfell Hall*

Anne had also become a teacher. From 1840, she was governess to the young girls of a wealthy family near York. Her employers, the Robinsons, were pleased with her and, perhaps noticing she was homesick, gave her a spaniel puppy. Anne named the pup "Flossy" and it followed her everywhere. In 1843, Mrs Robinson, in need of a tutor for their young son, Edmund, suggested Anne invite Branwell to fill the post. All seemed to go well – perhaps too well, for in the summer of 1845, a secret came to light: our charming brother Branwell had been flirting with Mrs Robinson! Imagine Anne's embarrassment; she and Branwell left their employers and came home to Haworth, bringing Flossy with them.

Poets 1846

"Literature cannot be the business of a woman's life: and it ought not to be." Robert Southey, then Poet Laureate, in a letter to Charlotte Brontë

So we sisters were all together again. One day I found a notebook of Emily's poems. Then Anne showed some of hers, so we decided we must all try to be published as poets – whatever Robert Southey might have said. At first Emily refused, until we had the idea of using made-up names. So Currer (me), Acton (Anne) and Ellis (Emily) Bell were born! In May of 1846 our poems were published to kind reviews. We only sold 2 copies of our collection, however it amused us that everyone presumed we were men.

And I will be Currer Bell...

What is she writing? Watch her now,
How fast her fingers move!
How eagerly her youthful brow
is bent in thought above!
Her long curls, drooping, shade the light,
She puts them quick aside,
Nor knows that band of crystals bright,
Her hasty touch untied.
It slips adown her silken dress,
Falls glittering at her feet;
Unmarked it falls, for she no less
Pursues her labour sweet.

Jane Eyre

"I am no bird; and no net ensnares me: I am a free human being with an independent will."
Charlotte Brontë, *Jane Eyre*

We had all begun writing novels by now. My first novel, *The Professor*, was turned down by every publisher I sent it to, until one publisher wrote me an encouraging letter. I was just finishing a second novel by then; a story of an orphan facing cruelty and blood-curdling terror. I sent it to them and they liked it. *Jane Eyre* was published a few months later and became a great success.

3) Jane finally leaves the school to become the governess to a little French girl, Adele, at Thornfield Hall, a gloomy Yorkshire mansion house.

4) Jane finds Adele charming. She also m the housekeeper and a mysterious servant named Grace Poole but her employer, Adele guardian, is away.

1) 10-year-old Jane Eyre is an orphan living with her aunt. The aunt and her children bully Jane, terrifying her by locking her in the room where her uncle died. They send her away to a charity school run by another bully, Mr Brocklehurst. Jane soon finds that school discipline is harsh but she befriends an older girl, Helen Burns. When Jane accidentally breaks her slate, Mr Brocklehurst stands her on a stool, and brands her a liar.

NO!

Take her away to the red room and lock her in there.

Avoid her company, this girl is - a liar!

2) Cold and badly treated many pupils fall ill. In a heartbreaking scene, Jane's friend Helen dies with Jane by her side. Only when Mr Brocklehurst's cruelty is discovered do conditions at the school improve.

5) One day Jane is out walking when a horseman gallops by. His horse rears and throws him.

Jane helps him but he is rude. Later, back at Thornfield, she discovers the horseman is her employer, Mr Rochester. At first they argue but he soon begins to enjoy Jane's sincerity. And Jane begins to fall in love ...

Is there a flood?

No, sir, but ther has been a fire

6) Jane hears strange noises at night and thinks it might be Grace Poole. When Mr Rochester's room catches fire one night, Jane saves his life. Later, an uninvited guest, Mr Mason, is wounded by someone, or something. Who is Mr Mason?

"Forgive me..."

"I am no bird; and no net ensnares me."

"Oh, Jane, you torture me!"

7) On her deathbed, Jane's aunt confesses that when Jane's rich uncle in Madeira, John Eyre, had wanted Jane to live with him and be heiress to his fortune she wrote back and told him that Jane was dead . . .

8) Back at Thornfield, Jane tells of her love to Mr Rochester. To her amazement, he proposes marriage. She writes to her Uncle John, saying she is alive and is to be married.

12) A young clergyman, St John finds Jane a teaching job at a village school. Then he learns Jane's true identity and reveals they are cousins. Their mutual uncle, John Eyre, has now died leaving Jane everything. She shares the fortune with her cousins but when St John asks her to marry him she refuses.

"We are cousins."

Jane!
Jane!
Jane!

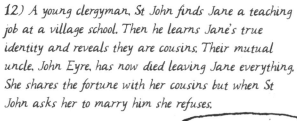

13) Suddenly she seems to hear Rochester's voice in the wind, calling her name.

"Mr Rochester has a wife now living!"

9) But during the wedding ceremony, Mr Mason turns up again. He says Rochester cannot marry because he is already married – to Mr Mason's sister! She is a madwoman, locked in the attic and cared for by Grace Poole.

10) Rochester explains he was tricked into marrying his wife, unaware of her madness. He keeps her safe upstairs rather than sending her away to a cruel institution.

11) Heartbroken, Jane runs far away until exhausted and near death she is found and nursed back to health by St John Rivers and his sisters, Diana and Mary.

"Reader, I married him."

"I am no better than the old lightning-struck chestnut-tree."

"You are no ruin, sir – no lightning-struck tree: you are green and vigorous."

14) Jane rushes back to Thornfield to find a burnt out ruin. Rochester's wife had set the house on fire. She died, but in his rescue attempts, Rochester lost a hand and his eyesight. After they marry he eventually recovers enough sight to see their baby son.

Wuthering Heights

"The angels were so angry that they flung me out ... on the top of Wuthering Heights; where I woke sobbing for joy." Emily Brontë, *Wuthering Heights*

Only Emily could have written this dark, romantic novel, set around a wind-blown farmhouse high on the moors. She was inspired by her love of wild places, her father's tales of Ireland and Tabby's local legends. She created a breathtaking story that both shocked and delighted her readers. There are a lot of deaths in this story – but people died young in those days; death and separation was a tragic fact of life.

1) Mr Lockwood visits his sullen landlord, Mr Heathcliff, at a remote moorland farmhouse called Wuthering Heights. A snowstorm forces him to stay the night in a little used room. Later he is awoken by the ghost of a girl trying to get into his window – is it a nightmare? Heathcliff rushes in. Lockwood decides to leave but, as he does, hears Heathcliff crying out "Cathy", inviting the ghost to return.

Let me in - let me in! I'm come home...

2) A servant, Nelly, tells Lockwood the tale: 30 years earlier, Mr Earnshaw, then the owner of Wuthering Heights, had returned from a trip to Liverpool with a street urchin he named Heathcliff. He brings him up like a son but his true son, Hindley, bullies the boy.

I found him lost and alone.

3) Heathcliff befriends Earnshaw's daughter, Catherine, and they spend hours together roaming the moors. They become inseparable.

4) When the kindly father dies, Hindley, now married, forces Heathcliff to be his servant. But Heathcliff and Catherine still meet to roam the moors. One night, they spy on the well-to-do Linton family at nearby Thrushcross Grange. When a guard dog bites Catherine, she stays as their guest while her leg heals.

5) When Catherine returns from the Lintons' she is much changed and mocks Heathcliff for being scruffy. She is clearly taken with Edgar Linton of Thrushcross Grange. Meanwhile, Hindley's wife has a baby boy, Hareton, but she dies soon after. Hindley turns to drink.

It would degrade me to marry Heathcliff...

Nelly, I AM Heathcliff - he's always, ALWAYS in my mind...

I would degrade her?

6) Heathcliff overhears Catherine telling Nelly she has agreed to marry Edgar. He runs away not hearing the end of the conversation when Catherine says she cannot live without him.

9) Isabella flees to London and has a baby, Linton. After she dies Heathcliff brings his son to Wuthering Heights. Years pass, the new generation become teenagers. After young Cathy befriends Linton, Heathcliff imprisons her and Nelly at Wuthering Heights until she marries Linton.

Stand off, or I shall knock you down.

Pappa wants us to marry.

You villain!

7) Heathcliff disappears. Catherine marries Edgar three years later and moves to Thruschross Grange. Suddenly Heathcliff returns, now a wealthy gentleman. He marries Edgar's sister, Isabella, to make Cathy jealous, and lodges at Wuthering Heights with drunken Hindley.

10) When sickly Linton also dies, Heathcliff forces Cathy to live with him at Wuthering Heights. Eventually Hareton befriends lonely Cathy, who teaches him to read.

Now, my bonny lad, we'll see if one tree won't grow as crooked as another, with the same wind to twist it!

11) Finally, madness takes hold of Heathcliff and he dies in the room where Lockwood saw Catherine's ghost.

Oh my heart's darling, hear me this time.

What is the matter, my little man?

12) Hareton and Cathy fall in love and marry. The story ends with Nelly meeting a shepherd boy who has seen the ghosts of Catherine and Heathcliff, now together at last as peaceful spirits on the moors.

There's Heathcliff and a woman yonder ... un' I darnut pass'em.

8) Catherine grows ill, torn between Heathcliff and Edgar. She dies but a baby survives her and is also named Catherine. Bitter and twisted, Heathcliff lets Hindley drink himself to death. He then takes possession of Wuthering Heights and Hareton who he treats cruelly as an unpaid, uneducated servant.

The Tenant of Wildfell Hall

"I am satisfied that if a book is good one, it is so whatever the sex of the author may be."
Anne Brontë, *The Tenant of Wildfell Hall*

Anne's first novel, *Agnes Grey*, based on her own unhappy experiences as a governess, was popular but her second novel, *The Tenant of Wildfell Hall*, published in 1848 and beginning with the famous words, "You must go back with me to the autumn of 1827" was to become her masterwork. In fact the first printing sold out within six weeks of publication.

3) One evening Gilbert spies on Mr Lawrence and Helen talking together and becomes jealous. Later, on meeting Mr Lawrence, he loses his temper and attacks him with his riding whip causing Lawrence to fall unconscious from his horse.

1) Gilbert Markham, a young farmer writes a series of letters telling the story of a mysterious widow, Helen Graham, a reclusive artist who, with her little son, moves into Wildfell Hall, an old and partly ruined mansion house on the moors.

2) Helen is unfriendly at first, and although Gilbert eventually befriends her and her little boy Arthur, she still keeps a distance between them and won't allow him to court her. Gilbert suspects she and his friend Mr Lawrence may be lovers, after rumours and gossip spread around the village.

4) Helen is angry, but eventually, she gives Gilbert her own diaries so he can read her story. The diaries tell him Helen isn't a widow. She has fled from her husband, who has ill-treated her. Gilbert also realises Mr Lawrence is her brother and not her lover.

5) Gilbert reads on: After the birth of their son, Helen's husband, Arthur Huntingdon, became jealous, accusing the baby of taking Helen's affections. He invited his friends to drink and gamble; then Helen discovered he was being unfaithful with another married woman, Lady Lowborough.

7) After reading the diary, Gilbert visits Helen. She admits her feelings for him, but then, when she returns to care for her dying husband, they lose touch. Time passes, and one day Gilbert hears that Helen, now a widow, is to remarry. He goes down to see the wedding and is relieved to discover it is her brother Mr Lawrence who is getting married.

6) Her husband made no secret of his mistress; worse still, he encouraged their little boy Arthur to drink and swear. Eventually, with help from her brother, Helen escaped to live secretly at Wildfell Hall supporting herself by selling her paintings.

8) Helen is now very wealthy and Gilbert presumes her too rich to want to marry a humble farmer. One day he travels to see her house and, by chance, bumps into her and Arthur. Delighted to be together again, she gives him a rose - he proposes to her and they marry.

39

London

"No coward soul is mine." Emily Brontë

One day it came to our attention that one publisher was saying that the Bells were really just one person who had written all of our novels – that was a step too far. Although Emily would not come with us, Anne and I took a train to London as soon as we could and marched straight into my publisher's office. They couldn't believe their eyes when they realised who we were! Once my publisher had got over the shock, he was very kind and gentlemanly. Together with his sisters, he took us to the opera and art galleries. We were not dressed for the opera having only our travel clothes – but we enjoyed ourselves immensely.

We noticed that fashionable Londoners sniggered at our out-of-date clothes, but we didn't care!

Safely back home by the kitchen fire, we told Emily and Tabby of our incredible London adventures.

41

Tragedy 1848 - 49

"I'm sure I should be myself were I once among the heather on those hills. Open the window again wide ..." Emily Brontë, *Wuthering Heights*

This part of my story is the hardest for me to tell . . . In the September of 1848, poor Branwell died of tuberculosis. Then, only a few weeks later, it took hold of my dearest, darling Emily. I feared the worst as soon as I saw her lying on the sofa, too weak to walk on her beloved moors and yet refusing the doctor. Stubbornly she hung on to life until just before Christmas and then, unbelievably, she was gone. At her funeral the lines from a poem of hers came into my mind.

Come walk with me,
come walk with me,
We were not once so few;
But Death has stolen our company,
As sunshine steals the dew.
He took them one by one and we
Are left, the only two ...

Keeper, Emily's faithful dog, came to the funeral and sat in the pews. He howled for days outside Emily's bedroom door after her death.

But that wasn't the end of tragedy; within months the illness returned mercilessly for Anne. Ellen and I took her on a last holiday to the seaside town of Scarborough before she died. To save Father going through the tragedy of burying another of his children we arranged for her to be buried there near the sea she loved so much.

Marriage 1854

"The trouble is not that I am single and likely to stay single, but that I am lonely and likely to stay lonely." Charlotte Brontë

Although our books were now best sellers, fame brought uninvited visitors to Haworth, even to church on Sundays to get a glimpse of me. Without my dear sisters, life at the parsonage grew very lonely. One evening, I was sitting in the dining room when my father's assistant, Arthur Bell Nicholls, walked in. I guessed his business as soon as I saw him shaking like a leaf. He asked me to marry him. When I told Father, he flew into a rage and Mr Nicholls felt forced to take a new job near Pontefract, over 30 miles away. But lovelorn Mr Nicholls wrote me such beautiful letters that eventually I relented and we married. We spent our honeymoon in Ireland before settling at Haworth Parsonage alongside my father, where I lived for the rest of my life.

Filming Wuthering Heights 1967

"What's the matter child? Why do you cry? Are you lost?" BBC TV script

"And that, dear listener, is all I have to tell you," she said, standing up and smoothing down her crumpled skirt and patting my arm. She left me there, with the soft wind breathing through the moorland grass, the heather and the harebells; but as she walked away I caught her last whispered words:

"Well-well; the sad minutes are moving,
Though loaded with trouble and pain;
And some time the loved and the loving
Shall meet on the mountains again . . ."

Someone was shaking my arm: "You're on in fifteen minutes, sleepyhead!" grinned a production assistant, handing me a mug of tea. I was going to be on telly . . .

After nine months enjoying a happy marriage and fame as a writer, Charlotte became ill. She died in March 1855 and lies to this day, alongside most of her family, in the vault at Haworth church. Her husband remained at Haworth Parsonage and looked after Patrick Brontë who lived to be 84. The novels of the Brontë sisters have lived on to become classics, read and admired all over the world. They have been made into films, animations and comic strips as well as many TV productions, including the one mentioned in this book; the 1967 BBC2 production of 'Wuthering Heights' directed by Peter Sasdy and starring many famous actors, such as Ian McShane, Angela Scoular and Anne Stallybrass, not to mention a local Haworth schoolboy . . .

First published in Great Britain in 2016 by The Watts Publishing Group

Text and illustrations © Mick Manning and Brita Granström 2016

The right of Mick Manning and Brita Granström to be identified as the authors and illustrators of this work have been asserted in accordance with the Copyright, Design and Patents Act, 1988.

Mick and Brita made the illustrations for this book. Find out more at www.mickandbrita.com

Editor: Rachel Cooke; Design: Sophie Pelham after concept layouts by Mick and Brita;
Cover design: Peter Scoulding

Drawn on location in Haworth.
With thanks for the advice and expertise of Ann Dinsdale, Collections Manager at the Brontë Parsonage Museum. You can visit Haworth and the Brontë Parsonage Museum,
Church Street, Haworth, Keighley, BD22 8DR www.bronte.org.uk

A CIP catalogue record is available from the British Library.
HB ISBN: 978 1 4451 4731 4
Library ebook ISBN: 978 1 4451 4733 8

Printed in China.

Franklin Watts
An imprint of Hachette Children's Group
Part of The Watts Publishing Group
Carmelite House, 50 Victoria Embankment, London EC4Y 0DZ

An Hachette UK Company

www.hachette.co.uk • www.franklinwatts.co.uk

For Des and Muriel Manning

"And some time the loved and the loving
Shall meet on the mountains again…"

The quotes used in this book were taken from the following sources:
p4 *The Professor*, Chapter 22, Charlotte Brontë, 1857; p6 'A Little While, a Little While', Emily Brontë, 1838, published 1850; p9 Sermon, Patrick Brontë, 1824; p10 *Jane Eyre*, Chapter 4, Charlotte Brontë, 1847; p12 'Loud Without the Wind Was Roaring', Emily Brontë, 1838, published 1850; p14 'Retrospection', Charlotte Brontë, 1835; p15 *A Day at Parry's Palace* by Charlotte Brontë, 1830; p16 Letter from Mary Taylor to Elizabeth Gaskell, 1856; p18 'Dream of the West', Charlotte Brontë, 1837; p20 Preface to *Selections From Poems*, Ellis Bell, Charlotte Brontë, 1850; p22 *Shirley*, Chapter 12, Charlotte Brontë, 1849; p22 *Jane Eyre*, Chapter 10, Charlotte Brontë, 1847; p25 'Stanzas to…', Emily Brontë, 1839; p26 'Loud Without the Wind Was Roaring', Emily Brontë, 1838, published 1850; p26 'A Little While, a Little While', Emily Brontë, 1838; p28 *Jane Eyre*, Chapter 38, Charlotte Brontë, 1847; p31 *The Tenant of Wildfell Hall*, Chapter 9, Anne Brontë, 1848; p33 Letter from Robert Southey to Charlotte Brontë, 1837; p32 'Song', Emily Brontë, 1845; 'The Letter', Charlotte Brontë, 1848; A Gondal poem, Anne Brontë, 1845; p34 *Jane Eyre*, Chapter 23, Charlotte Brontë, 1847; p36 *Wuthering Heights*, Chapter 9, Emily Brontë, 1847; p38 *The Tenant of Wildfell Hall*, Preface, Anne Brontë, 1848; p40 'No Coward Soul Is Mine', Emily Brontë, 1846; p42 *Wuthering Heights*, Chapter 12, Emily Brontë, 1847; p43 'Come Walk With Me', Emily Brontë, undated; p46 'Loud Without the Wind Was Roaring', Emily Brontë, 1838, published 1850.

Mick and Brita used the following references and sources in the creation of this book:
The author's childhood memories; the Brontës' novels, various editions; the Brontës' childhood writings, various sources; poems of the Brontë Sisters, various publications; the Brontë Parsonage Museum, a personal tour with Ann Dinsdale; reference material kindly provided by the Brontë Parsonage Museum; Bradford Textiles Archive, a personal tour with Helen Farrar; visits to locations around Haworth and Bolton Abbey; *The Brontës of Haworth*, Ann Dinsdale; *The Brontës*, Juliet Barker; *The Life of Charlotte Brontë*, Elizabeth Gaskell; *The Art of the Brontës*, Alexander and Sellars; 'Wuthering Heights' DVD, BBC, directed by Peter Sasdy 1967; letters to the author from the BBC; image of Mick on TV taken by the his aunt, reproduced with permission from the BBC Archive/Getty Images. Every attempt has been made to clear copyright. Should there be any inadvertent omission, please apply to the Publishers for rectification.

THE BRITISH BROADCASTING CORPORATION

HEAD OFFICE: BROADCASTING HOUSE, LONDON, W.1

TELEVISION CENTRE: WOOD LANE, LONDON, W.12

TELEGRAMS: BROADCASTS LONDON TELEX * CABLES: BROADCASTS LONDON-W1 * TELEX: 22182
TELEPHONE: SHEPHERDS BUSH 8000   Ext. 2228/9

9th August, 1967

Dear Michael,

Thank you very much for appearing in WUTHERING HEIGHTS. I am only sorry that it took such a long time and that you got so cold but I hope the pocket money made up for it and that you will enjoy seeing yourself on the screen. Don't forget; 18th November is the day! Although I do hope you father will be able to arrange for you to see all the episodes. The first one goes out on BBC-2 on 28th October.

Again, many thanks for your help.

PAGE 44

ELLEN: What's the matter, child? Why do you cry? Are you lost?

ELLEN: Then what ails you?

BOY: It's Mr. Heathcliff …

ELLEN: Who?

BOY: Him and a woman. They's yonder, under the Crag, and I daren't pass them.